Tiana the Toy Fairy

by Daisy Meadows

ORCHARD

www.rainbowmagic.co.uk

Jack Frost's Spell

Tiana's magic makes me mad.
This world gets toys I never had.
Humans don't deserve such luck
So I will leave them thunderstruck.

Take that marble and run!
No human child will now have fun.
I'll take what's mine from girls and boys,
And fill my shelves with all their toys.

Contents

Autumn Adventure

"Did I mention that there are going to be giant toys and a toy train?" said Kirsty Tate, reading the leaflet for the tenth time since they had got into the car that morning.

"And a dressing-up house with toy costumes and a photo booth where we can get pictures of ourselves dressed up," said her best friend Rachel Walker, peering over Kirsty's shoulder. "This is going to be the best day *ever*."

"All the children in Wetherbury are thrilled that the Toy Town Funfair is coming," said Kirsty's mum, Mrs Tate. "It's a wonderful way to start the October half term."

Rachel, Kirsty and Kirsty's parents were driving towards Kirsty's home village of Wetherbury. They had picked Rachel up early and were planning to spend the whole day at the amazing funfair. It was coming to the town for one day only, and the local children hadn't been able to sleep for excitement.

"Some of the mums and dads are just as excited as the children," said Mr Tate, rubbing his hands together and glancing at the car clock. "Are we nearly there yet?"

Mrs Tate grinned at him. "Ten more minutes," she said.

Rachel and Kirsty bounced up and down in their seats and shared eager smiles. They had a whole day to spend at a funfair where everything was about toys. It seemed too good to be true.

"Who wants to hear me sing *Ten Green Bottles* again?" asked Mr Tate with mischief in his eyes.

"No, thank you," said Mrs Tate, laughing. "We've already heard it three times this morning."

Smiling, Mr Tate turned on the radio, which gave the girls a chance to talk without being overheard. And of course, the first thing they wanted to talk about was magic.

"This feels so incredibly amazing, it's almost as if we're on our way to Fairyland," Rachel whispered.

"I've got that same fluttery feeling in my tummy that I get when we turn into fairies."

"Me too," said Kirsty. "I wonder if we will see any of our fairy friends today. I'm sure they must love things like toy festivals and funfairs."

"As long as we don't see Jack Frost or any of his goblins, I'll be happy," Rachel replied.

The best friends were ordinary girls who shared an extraordinary secret. One day on Rainspell Island they had met a fairy. They had shared many magical adventures with her and her sisters, and now they were firm friends with all the fairies of Fairyland – as well as Queen Titania and King Oberon. Even though they had often visited Fairyland, it was always as exciting as if it were the very first time.

It was not just fairies that the girls had met on Rainspell Island. They had foiled the plans of Jack Frost, the King of the Goblins. He lived in a cold, gloomy castle in a dark corner of Fairyland, and he was always trying to spoil things for the fairies. Since that first meeting, the girls had often helped to save the fairies from Jack Frost and his naughty goblins.

Suddenly, Kirsty sat up very straight and still.

"Rachel, did you see that?" she asked.

Rachel hadn't seen anything, but she knew the look on Kirsty's face very well. It meant that Kirsty had seen something magical. Kirsty pointed at her mum's headrest and then Rachel saw it — a twinkling light, like sunshine sparkling on a stream. They both knew exactly what it meant. There was a fairy in the car!

A Thief in Toy Town

As Rachel and Kirsty watched, the light changed. It grew brighter, and then there was a multi-coloured flurry of sparkles and a puff of hundreds and thousands. More sweets rained down on the girls' laps, as a brand-new fairy appeared in front of them. She hovered behind the

headrest so that
Mr and Mrs
Tate couldn't
see her, and
waved. The
girls waved
back.

"How
can we
talk to
her without
your mum and dad
noticing?" asked Rachel in a low voice.

The radio was still on, and Mr and Mrs
Tate were chatting. Kirsty smiled.

"I've got an idea," she said.

She raised her knees and rested the
leaflet about the funfair on them,
standing it up. The fairy fluttered forward

and perched on Kirsty's knees, hidden from the grown-ups by the leaflet.

"Good thinking," said Rachel, using her finger to dab at the hundreds and thousands on her lap, and popping them into her mouth.

"Hello," said the little fairy. "I'm Tiana the Toy Fairy."

She had cheerful brown eyes that looked full of fun, and her untamed hair bounced on her shoulders as she bobbed up and down. She was wearing a pair of blue jeans and a white peplum T-shirt with a starry pink-and-purple cardigan.

"It's great to meet you, Tiana," said Kirsty. "Are you coming with us to Toy Town?"

"Yes," said Tiana with an anxious frown. "Oh dear, I've been so excited about today, but now it's all gone wrong. I'm really worried."

"What's the matter?" Rachel asked.

"I live in a place in Fairyland, also called Toy Town," Tiana explained. "It's the start of our annual toy festival today and I am supposed to make a speech at the opening ceremony. But when I left my house to get ready, something terrible happened. Jack Frost broke in and stole my magical marble so that he could have all toys for himself."

"That rotten Jack Frost," said Rachel, shaking her head. "Why does he always have to spoil things for everyone?"

"I have to get my magical marble back," said Tiana, clasping her hands together. "It looks after toys and good times everywhere, making sure that people have real fun with toys and are kind to each other while they're playing.

21

Without it, toys will stop working the way they should, and the Toy Town Festival will go badly wrong. The Wetherbury funfair will be ruined too. Please, will you help me?"

"Yes, of course," said Kirsty at once. "Tiana, if Jack Frost wants to gather all toys for himself, I bet he'll start at the human Toy Town."

"And here we are," Rachel added, as the car pulled into Wetherbury car park and stopped.

Tiana dived out of sight into Kirsty's pocket as Mr Tate switched the radio off and turned to the girls.

"Here's a bit of money for games and rides," he said, handing each of them a little purse. "Have fun, and we'll meet you in the Wetherbury Café for lunch."

Rachel and Kirsty thanked him and jumped out of the car. They could hardly wait to start exploring!

None of the Fun of the Fair

With Tiana still tucked safely in Kirsty's pocket, the girls joined the crowds of other families on their way to the funfair. They heard its cheery music first, and then squealed in delight when they saw what was waiting for them.

It looked as if a brand-new town had sprung up in the middle of Wetherbury, with brightly coloured tents, bunting strung from roof to roof in every colour of the rainbow, and kites swooping and diving overhead. A Ferris wheel, swing boats and a red-and-white helter skelter rose up between the tents. Everywhere

they looked, people were trying the
games, eating candyfloss and playing
with toys. People dressed up as toys were
dotted all around. Rachel and Kirsty
weaved through the funfair, calling out as
they spotted different characters.

"Look – a teddy bear and a rag doll,"
said Rachel, pulling Kirsty towards them.

"Over here — a Jack-in-the-Box and a tin soldier," said Kirsty, pulling her best friend in the opposite direction.

They collapsed in a heap and giggled as a giant silver robot stopped and looked down at them.

"Hello," said Rachel, kneeling up and brushing the grass off her skirt. "Do you work here at the funfair?"

"Mind your own business," snapped the robot.

28

"Get up and stop messing around."

He stomped away and Kirsty and Rachel exchanged shocked glances.

"That wasn't very nice," said Kirsty.

As they stood up, they saw the teddy bear wagging his finger crossly at a group of children. One of the little girls started to cry, and the teddy bear put his hands on his hips.

"She was only playing with her ball," said a little boy, putting his arm around the girl.

"She should only play with the toys that are sold *here*," the teddy shouted.

A loud shout made Kirsty and Rachel turn around. There was a long queue of people at the coconut shy behind them, but the attendant was closing it up.

"No more games," he said. "Someone has taken all my coconuts."

Rachel and Kirsty turned slowly on the spot, looking carefully at the games and rides around them. The jolly music was still playing, but no one seemed to be having a good time. Visitors were arguing with attendants, games were not working as they should and the toy train had broken down. There were tubs of toys for

everyone to play with, but the children
beside them had tear-stained faces.

"These toys are all broken," wailed a
little boy as his mother
cuddled him.

A teenage
girl pushed her
candyfloss into a
bin nearby.

"There's something
wrong with it," the
girls heard her
say. "It tastes like
bogeys."

"This is all because
the magical marble is
missing," Kirsty said. "Not a single toy
or game or ride is making people happy
right now."

"All except one," said Rachel. "Look over there. That entertainer in the big hat seems to be doing just fine."

The entertainer was wearing a colourful top hat with a wide brim that hid his face. Sweets and toys were dangling from his hat, and a cheering, noisy crowd surrounded him as he capered around. He was playing games and handing out yummy-looking treats as prizes.

"They all seem happy," said Kirsty. "I wonder why."

"Look at the crowd more closely," whispered Tiana, peeping out from Kirsty's pocket.

The girls looked again, and then they both gasped. Everyone in the crowd was wearing a cap, but their enormous feet gave them away at once.

"They're *goblins*," said Rachel. "What are we going to do?"

The Silliest Goblin

Rachel and Kirsty hurried closer to the crowd of goblins.

"Is Jack Frost among them?" Tiana asked in a muffled voice.

"I don't think so," Kirsty replied. "I'm just trying to see if any of the goblins has a bag. They might be carrying your magical marble."

Just then, the entertainer threw back his head and laughed, and the girls were able to see his face.

"Jack Frost!" they said together.

Tiana poked her head out of Kirsty's pocket in alarm.

"Oh no," she cried. "Look at the things that are dangling from his hat."

"I can see a lollipop, a teddy, some sweets," Rachel said, watching as Jack Frost turned his head. "And – oh my goodness – a marble."

"*My* marble," said Tiana sadly.

"Don't worry," said Kirsty at once. "We'll get it back. Can you disguise us as goblins?"

Tiana looked shocked, and Rachel smiled at her.

"Don't worry," she said. "We've done it before, and we know how to act like goblins. Hopefully we can get close enough to get your marble back."

They slipped under the canvas of the closed coconut shy, and Tiana fluttered out of Kirsty's pocket. She raised her wand.

"Are you really sure about this?" she asked nervously.

"Yes," said Kirsty. "It's the best and quickest way to get to your magical marble. Don't worry, Tiana. We'll be OK."

Rachel squeezed her hand as Tiana cast the spell. The girls felt themselves changing shape at once. Their skin became knobbly and green, and their noses and fingers grew long and thin. Kirsty lifted her enormous feet one after the other.

"I always feel as if I'm going to trip over when I'm a goblin," she laughed, grabbing Rachel's arm for balance.

"Don't forget to put on a goblin voice," Rachel reminded her.

"Of course," said Kirsty, using a squawky, whiny voice.

Tiana stifled a giggle. "You look and sound perfect," she said. "I will stay in here and watch until you come back. Good luck, Rachel and Kirsty."

Wearing wide-brimmed caps just like the real goblins, Rachel and Kirsty hurried over to join the group. They jumped and ran around Jack Frost, squawking as loudly as all the others.

"Our next game is 'Who's the Silliest Goblin?' said Jack Frost, glaring at them all through his narrow eyes. "You all have to be as silly as you can. The biggest nincompoop of all will win a prize from the pile."

He waved his hands to a pile of toys, sweets and games on the grass behind him. Unlike the toys in the tubs, these all looked as if they were working properly.

The goblins started pulling silly faces, making ridiculous noises and shouting out nonsense words. Jack Frost pointed at them and cackled with laughter.

"You're all idiots," he said. "But the biggest fool of the lot is you, warty. You win a train."

A goblin whose nose was covered in warts stepped forward, puffing out his chest with pride. Jack Frost threw a toy train at him, but  it disappeared as soon as it was in the goblin's hands. Jack Frost sniggered.

"That should train you not to believe everything you're told," he said, flinging some sugar mice into the crowd.

"Next we have a competition to find out who can flatter me the most."

As the goblins started shouting out compliments, Rachel took a bite of the sugar mouse she had caught.

"The goblins don't realise that his games are really mean," she said. "Oh, yuck! This sugar mouse tastes horrible."

"So does mine," said Kirsty. "But all the goblins seem to love them."

"It must be because he has the magical marble," said Rachel. "No one notices because the magic makes it seem fun."

"Then why do *we* notice?" asked Kirsty.

"Maybe it's because we know the *real* purpose of the marble," said Rachel. "It's supposed to help people have real fun with toys and be kind to each other, not to make fun of people."

The other goblins were still calling out nice things about Jack Frost, trying to win the next prize.

"I've got an idea," said Rachel. "If we join in with the competition, maybe we can get close enough to grab the marble."

Using their sharp goblin elbows to push through the crowd, Rachel and Kirsty started to shout out compliments.

"Your beard is the pointiest!" Kirsty hollered. "You are the iciest and the scariest!"

"I like your spiky hair," said Rachel. "It

suits you. You should take off your hat so we can see it properly."

Jack Frost turned to glare at her. "Don't tell marvellous *me* what to do!" he boomed angrily.

The girls groaned. How could they persuade him to take off his hat?

"I've got an idea!" said Kirsty. "Tiana, could you magic up an even fancier one? Perhaps we could convince Jack Frost to switch hats."

"Of course," said Tiana. "I know just the thing..."

Flight to Fairyland

Rachel and Kirsty saw a ribbon of
fairy dust ripple out of the coconut
shy, snake through the grass and wrap
around the pile of prizes on the ground.
A magnificent, multi-coloured top hat
appeared on the pile. It was made of red
and purple velvet stripes, with tiny green

goblins decorating the brim.

"Wow," said a goblin next to Rachel. "Is that the next prize?"

"I want to win that hat," said another goblin, leapfrogging over Kirsty.

Everyone had stopped gazing at Jack Frost. Instead, they were all gawping at the amazing hat. The girls did the same, so they didn't stand out, and Jack Frost glared at them all.

"You're supposed to be praising *me*," he hissed through gritted teeth. "Get on with it!"

There was no reply. All the goblins had gathered around the hat. Jack Frost started juggling. He pulled five toy bunnies out of his ears. He turned one goblin's hat into a flowerpot. But still the goblins paid him no attention. Rachel and Kirsty edged closer to Jack Frost, trying not to be noticed.

"Fine," he said, stomping towards the prizes and flinging goblins aside. He tore his hat from his head and dived for the new one.

"This is our chance!" said Rachel.

She darted over to grab the old hat, while the goblins fought with each other, trying to pull the new hat away from Jack Frost.

"Got it!" cried Rachel, starting to run to Tiana.

But the warty goblin had been watching her. He stuck out his leg and cackled as she tripped. The

hat sailed through the air and Rachel landed with a thump. When she looked up, Jack Frost was standing in front of her, his old hat in his hand.

"You've got some explaining to do," he said, tapping his foot. "Start talking, wart face."

Kirsty hurried over to stand beside Rachel, and then they saw Tiana peeping out from the coconut shy. She raised her wand and sent another magical ribbon of fairy dust rippling towards them. Instantly, the girls were transformed into humans again.

"You!" shouted Jack Frost, shaking his fist at them. "I should have guessed that

you pesky humans would try to spoil
things for me."

He rammed the hat
on his head and the
dangling objects
shook around his
snarling face.

"Give Tiana's
marble back,"
said Kirsty
bravely.

"No way," Jack
Frost replied. "I've had it
with you and your silly human world."

There was a bolt of icy magic and
a puff of blue smoke, and Jack Frost
disappeared with all his goblins. Tiana
shot out of the coconut shy and hid
herself under a lock of Rachel's hair.

"He must have taken my magical marble back to Fairyland," she said. "What am I going to do? The Toy Town Festival is about to start – everything will be ruined."

The girls felt sorry for Tiana.

"Take us with you to Fairyland," said Rachel at once. "Somehow, we'll find him before the opening ceremony. Let's go!"

There was a flurry of multi-coloured sparkles, and everything around them disappeared. Suddenly they were standing

on a grand stage, surrounded by more
toys than the girls had ever seen in one
place. Gauzy wings fluttered on their
backs.

"Welcome to the Toy Town Festival,"
said Tiana, twirling around so fast that
she lifted off the ground.

"It looks amazing," said Kirsty. She
turned to stare at a whole town full
of stalls, rides and games. There was a
stall selling every type of toy ever made.
Bunting and streamers fluttered in the
breeze. But all the fairies who were
crowding around the festival looked sad.

"There's Lottie the Lollipop Fairy," said
Rachel, fluttering over to the sweetshop
stall. "Hi, Lottie! It's great to see you."

Lottie hugged her.

"It's great to see you too," she said. "I just wish the festival was as much fun as usual. The opening ceremony is about to start, but no one is feeling excited."

Maddie the Playtime Fairy came over to the girls.

"It's so sad," said Maddie. "You've worked so hard to organise this festival, Tiana. And now none of the games are working and no one is having fun – all because of mean Jack Frost."

She stared over Rachel's shoulder and they all turned around. Jack Frost was leaning against a teddy-bear stall, watching all the sad-looking fairies and laughing so hard that his hat was wobbling.

"That's it!" cried Tiana.

And she zoomed towards Jack Frost.

Laughter Saves the Day

"Tiana!" cried Maddie and Lottie in alarm.

"Come back!" called Rachel and Kirsty.

Jack Frost looked astonished to see Tiana coming towards him. His mouth fell open as she stopped in front of him and smiled. Rachel and Kirsty landed behind her.

"Are you going to shout at me?" he asked, taking a step back.

"Why would I want to shout on the day of the Toy Town Festival?" Tiana said. "After all, toys are happy things. They should make you giggle."

She reached out her
hand and gave
Jack Frost a
gentle tickle.

"Tee hee!"
said Jack
Frost, and his
hat wobbled
again. One of
the lollipops fell
off it.

"Do you know
what the polar bear said to the penguin?"
Tiana asked. "*Ice* to see you."

Jack Frost laughed again, even harder,
and a sweet fell off his hat. Rachel and
Kirsty exchanged an excited glance.
Suddenly they understood exactly what
Tiana was trying to do.

"How do you start a teddy bear race?" Rachel asked. "Ready, teddy, go!"

Jack Frost snorted with laughter and another lollipop fell from his hat.

"What do you call a cold robot?" asked Kirsty. "A snow-bot!"

With a loud guffaw, Jack Frost's hat wobbled wildly and the magical marble fell off and tumbled to the ground. Tiana darted forwards and pounced on the marble.

"Cheat!" Jack Frost roared. "Trickster!"

But his voice was drowned out under
a sudden swell of cheering and laughter.
The rides were working, the games were
fun again, and all the fairies were smiling
and happy. Trumpets sounded, and
then King Oberon and Queen Titania
appeared on the stage in a flurry of
purple sparkles.

"Welcome to the Toy Town Festival,"
said Queen Titania with a smile. "I
would like to invite Tiana to the stage to
open the event."

She waved her wand,
and a red silk
ribbon appeared,
strung across
the stage.
Tiana flew up
to the stage,
and turned
to face the
smiling crowd.

"Thank you,
Your Majesties,"
she said. "Please could
I share the ribbon-cutting with two very
special friends?"

Everyone knew exactly who she meant, and all the fairies cheered as Rachel and Kirsty flew up to the stage. They curtsied to the king and queen.

"Thank you, dear Rachel and Kirsty," said Queen Titania. "Once again you have helped us and been wonderful friends to Fairyland. We are lucky to know you."

Rachel and Kirsty felt their cheeks go red.

"It's us who are lucky," Rachel said. "Thank you for being our friends."

The fairies in the crowd clapped and waved. Rachel and Kirsty waved back, seeing many of their friends. Then they picked up the scissors and cut the ribbon. The toy festival was open!

Rachel and Kirsty shared a smile and gazed down at

68

the happy crowd, who were laughing,
dancing and playing with all the
amazing toys. Then they felt Tiana's arms
slip around their waists.

"Your own Toy Town Funfair is waiting
for you," she said. "Thank you for all
your help today. Without you, there
would be no toy
festival here and
no funfair in
your world."

"We were
so happy to
help," said
Kirsty.

They shared
a big hug,
and then Tiana
raised her wand.

There was a whoosh of multi-coloured sparkles, and then the girls were standing in the middle of the Wetherbury funfair, human once again. As usual when they had been in Fairyland, no time had passed in the human world.

"We've come back at exactly the same

moment we left, but everything looks different," said Rachel.

All around them were happy smiling faces and the sound of laughter. The people dressed up as toys were dancing through the funfair, the toy train was steaming along the track and the photo booth was working perfectly.

"Kirsty! Rachel!" Mr and Mrs Tate appeared, both wearing clown noses and giggling. The girls burst into laughter.

"This is the best funfair ever. Are you enjoying yourselves?" asked Mrs Tate.

"Yes," said Kirsty, squeezing Rachel's hand and smiling. "We're having a truly *magical* time!"

The End

Now it's time for Kirsty and Rachel to help...

Susie the Sister Fairy

Read on for a sneak peek...

The driveway of Golden Trumpet Adventure Camp was packed with cars.

"There's Kirsty," shouted Rachel Walker, jumping up and down as she saw her best friend's car drive up and park.

Kirsty Tate scrambled out of the back and dashed towards Rachel.

"I'm so excited about this week I can't stop thinking about it," said Kirsty as they shared a hug. "I even think about it in my dreams."

"I can confirm that she hasn't talked about anything else for weeks," said Mrs Tate, carrying Kirsty's rucksack over to them. "I'm so glad that we saw the camp advertised in the local newspaper."

"It was a brilliant idea, Mum," said Kirsty.

Rachel and Kirsty hugged each other again. Golden Trumpet Adventure Camp was exactly halfway between their homes in Wetherbury and Tippington. When Mrs Tate had suggested it, the girls had agreed that it was the perfect place to spend some time together.

Looking around, they saw a big wooden building behind them, with a big sign over the door.

Golden Trumpet Adventure Camp Dining Cabin and Offices

A forest surrounded the dining cabin, and the sound of birdsong filled the air. A young man jogged over to them with a warm smile.

"Hi, I'm Tristan," he said. "I'm one of the camp leaders. It's our job to look after you while you're here and make sure you have a great time."

Rachel and Kirsty introduced themselves and Tristan checked their names on a list.

"You'll be staying in Maple Cabin," he said. "You will be sharing it with two other girls, but they haven't arrived yet. Follow me and I'll take you there."

The girls said goodbye to their parents, picked up their rucksacks and followed Tristan into the leafy forest. The winding trail was so narrow that they had to walk in single file.

"The forest is full of trails like this," Tristan said. "This one is the quickest way from your cabin to the dining cabin."

"What sort of things will we be doing this week?" Rachel asked.

"Too many for me to remember," said Tristan with a grin. "There's horseriding, waterskiing, hide-and-seek, obstacle courses, climbing, cycling – it's going to be great fun. Here we are – welcome to Maple Cabin."

Read **Susie the Sister Fairy** to find out what adventures are in store for Kirsty and Rachel!

RAINBOW magic

Calling all parents, carers and teachers!
The Rainbow Magic fairies are here to help
your child enter the magical world of reading.
Whatever reading stage they are at, there's
a Rainbow Magic book for everyone!
Here is Lydia the Reading Fairy's guide to
supporting your child's journey at all levels.

1

Starting Out
Our Rainbow Magic Beginner Readers are perfect for first-time readers who are just beginning to develop reading skills and confidence. Approved by teachers, they contain a full range of educational levelling, as well as lively full-colour illustrations.

2

Developing Readers
Rainbow Magic Early Readers contain longer stories and wider vocabulary for building stamina and growing confidence. These are adaptations of our most popular Rainbow Magic stories, specially developed for younger readers in conjunction with an Early Years reading consultant, with full-colour illustrations.

3

Going Solo
The Rainbow Magic chapter books – a mixture of series and one-off specials – contain accessible writing to encourage your child to venture into reading independently. These highly collectible and much-loved magical stories inspire a love of reading to last a lifetime.

www.rainbowmagicbooks.co.uk

"Rainbow Magic got my daughter reading chapter books. Great sparkly covers, cute fairies and traditional stories full of magic that she found impossible to put down" – Mother of Edie (6 years)

"Florence LOVES the Rainbow Magic books. She really enjoys reading now" – Mother of Florence (6 years)

The Rainbow Magic Reading Challenge

Well done, fairy friend – you have completed the book!
This book was worth 5 points.

See how far you have climbed on the
Reading Rainbow opposite.

The more books you read, the more points you will get,
and the closer you will be to becoming a Fairy Princess!

Do you want your own Reading Rainbow?
1. Cut out the coin below
2. Go to the Rainbow Magic website
3. Download and print out your poster
4. Add your coin and climb up the Reading Rainbow!

There's all this and lots more at
www.rainbowmagicbooks.co.uk

You'll find activities, competitions, stories, a special
newsletter and complete profiles of all the
Rainbow Magic fairies. Find a fairy with your name!